Hoppy
EASTER

Other books by Patricia Hermes
you will enjoy:

My Secret Valentine
Something Scary
Turkey Trouble
Christmas Magic

Hoppy
EASTER

Patricia Hermes

Illustrated by
Amy Wummer

A
LITTLE APPLE
PAPERBACK

SCHOLASTIC INC.
New York Toronto London Auckland Sydney

ISBN 0-590-38365-5

Text copyright © 1998 by Patricia Hermes.
Illustrations copyright © 1998 by Scholastic Inc.
All rights reserved. Published by Scholastic Inc.
LITTLE APPLE PAPERBACKS and associated logos are trademarks and/or registered trademarks of Scholastic Inc.

12 11 10 9 8 7 6 5 4   8 9/9 0 1 2 3/0

Printed in the U.S.A.   40

First Scholastic printing, March 1998

For my friend Patricia Reilly Giff

Contents

Hoppy EASTER

1

The Baby Bunny

"Look out, Obie!" Katie yelled to her twin brother, Obidiah. "Out of my way!"

But it was too late.

Katie was racing down the hill on her bike and she couldn't stop.

Obie was at the bottom of the hill on his bike. He moved, but not fast enough.

Katie bumped right into him.

And she and Obie ended up in a jumble on the ground.

Katie sat up. "Are you all right, Obie?" she asked.

"You ran into me," Obie said.

"I didn't mean to," Katie said. "I skidded. Are you all right?"

"I'm all right," Obie said. He rubbed his elbow.

Katie got up and brushed herself off. She looked at Obie.

He was still rubbing his elbow.

"Is it cut?" Katie said.

"You look," Obie answered.

He pulled up the sleeve of his shirt and held out his arm. But he didn't look.

Katie bent over his arm. No blood. Just a red place and a little dirt.

Katie was glad that there was no blood. Obie was a little scared of blood. Actually, Obie was a little scared of lots of things. But that was all right with Katie. Obie was her twin brother and her favorite brother. He was a lot nicer than her older brothers, Sam and Matt. They were big pains. And he was a lot nicer than her baby brother, Baby-Child. Baby-Child's real name was Joshua but everybody called him

2

Baby-Child. He was a big pain, too. Still, she loved them all. It was just that she loved Obie best of all.

She looked up at him. He was still holding out his arm and his eyes were closed.

"You can look now," Katie said. "No blood."

Obie took a deep breath. He looked down at his arm. "Oh, good," he said.

Katie helped Obie pull down his sleeve. Then she looked all around.

Obie looked around, too.

They were in their backyard, but way, way down in back where the woods began. It was very early. The sun was just coming up. They weren't supposed to be out so early but they had snuck out. Because Katie had something very important to do.

"Katie?" Obie said. "Do you really think we can catch him?"

Katie nodded. "We can," she said.

"But bunnies are very, very fast," Obie said.

"Not when they get caught up in a cage," Katie said.

Obie frowned. He made a very big, worried face. He didn't say anything more, though.

"Come on," Katie said. "Let's do it."

She went over to her bike and wiggled the basket hard. She knew it would come off. It always did. She wiggled it more and more until it came loose. Then she carried the basket back to the big tree she had almost crashed into on her bike. She crouched down on the ground by the tree.

There was a tiny little hole in the ground by the tree. The night before, she and Obie had seen a bunny run down that hole — a tiny, brown, fluffy baby bunny. A bunny that Katie needed to have.

Katie bent over and peeked down into the hole.

But she couldn't see a bunny. Actually, she couldn't see anything. Not anything but a big, dark hole.

She sat up on her heels. Then she

took the bike basket. She put the basket upside down over the hole.

"See?" Katie said. "It's all set. When he comes up, he comes right out into that basket. And I'll be here to catch him."

"What if he doesn't come up?" Obie said.

"He will," Katie said. "As soon as the sun comes up."

"What if he runs right back down again?" Obie said.

"Oh, I almost forgot!" Katie said.

She dug in the pocket of her jeans. She pulled out a carrot, kind of limp-looking. "See?" she said, and she put the carrot inside the basket. "As soon as he sees this or smells it, he'll stay here to eat it."

Obie sighed. "Know what?" he said. "I don't think bunnies like to get catched."

"Caught," Katie said.

"That's what I said," Obie said. "I don't think they like that."

"They do," Katie said.

"I wouldn't if I was a bunny," Obie said. "I'd miss the other bunnies in my family."

"Oh," Katie said. She thought about that. Then she said, "They probably don't mind. Remember that book we read in class, *Rabbit Days*? That bunny liked being with a people family."

Obie didn't answer.

"Anyway," Katie said, "if you were a bunny, you'd be glad I caught you because I'd feed you lots and lots of carrots."

"I hate carrots," Obie said.

Katie made a face. "If you were a bunny, you'd like them," she said.

Obie just looked at his watch. Obie was always looking at his watch. He didn't like being late.

"It's six o'clock, Katie," Obie said after a while. "We have to go in soon to get ready for school."

"Soon," Katie said. "I know he'll come out soon."

"Katie?" Obie said. "Is it because of Tiffany you want the bunny so much?"

Katie just shrugged. "Maybe," she said.

She hadn't told Obie the reason she needed a bunny, but he was right. It was sort of because of Tiffany. She was bringing her pet rabbit to school for show-and-tell. Katie loved bunnies. Their class had a bunny once, but it got sick and died. Katie wished so much it hadn't died. She loved bunnies more than just about anything in the whole world. And now Tiffany had one. Tiffany said her bunny was big and white and fluffy. That was even its name — Fluffy the bunny. She said it was the prettiest rabbit ever.

Tiffany was always bragging. She was a big bragger, and a big pain. She was even a bigger pain than Baby-Child.

But if Katie could just catch this tiny baby bunny, then Tiffany wouldn't have the cutest rabbit of all.

Katie would.

2

Standing Straight and Tall

They waited and waited and waited, but the bunny never came out. Finally, Obie said they couldn't wait any longer or they'd be late for school.

Sometimes their teacher, Mrs. Henry, said no recess when they were late. Obie always got Katie to school on time. Well, almost always.

So Katie had to go to school without any bunny. She was very mad. Now Tiffany would have the best show-and-tell ever. And Katie had nothing special at all. The only thing she had was her baby Koala. Koala was special to Katie, but Katie didn't think he'd be special to anyone else. He was tiny and furry and he used to hang on to her pencils with his tight little paws. Now, though, all his fur was almost worn off from getting patted, and his paws were broken. He couldn't hang on much anymore.

Katie didn't know what to do. And she was sort of sad.

But when they got to school, Katie got very happy. Because Tiffany wasn't there! She was absent.

Katie looked over at Tiffany's desk. She looked in the coat closet at Tiffany's coat hook. No Tiffany.

Katie smiled. She went to her seat and leaned close to Amelia, her best friend. It was early morning, before pledge and before attendance. They were allowed to talk if they talked with inside voices. Katie used her quietest inside voice.

"Guess what?" she said to Amelia.

"What?" Amelia said. She smiled at Katie.

Katie smiled back at her. "Tiffany's absent," Katie said.

"Too bad," Amelia said.

"How come?" Katie asked.

"Because she was going to bring in a bunny," Amelia said. "I'd like to pat the bunny."

Katie didn't answer.

"Tiffany has good show-and-tell stuff," Amelia said.

"I do, too," Katie said.

"I know," Amelia said. She smiled at Katie again. "I liked it when you showed us Koala."

"Oh," Katie said.

She pulled her face into a big frown. She had forgotten she'd already shown Koala.

"I'm showing a funny head," Amelia said. "My grandpa brought it from some island. Want to see it?"

"Yeah, let's see!" Emil said.

Katie looked around.

Emil Marks had snuck up on the other side of Amelia's desk and was leaning over it. Katie liked Emil, even though he was always talking about his grandma and bragging about her. Katie got sick of his bragging sometimes. Still, she thought she knew why he did it. It was because Emil had no mother or father. He lived with his grandma. Katie thought it must be hard to have no mother or father. And mostly, she liked Emil.

Amelia didn't like Emil, though. She didn't like any boys, although Katie knew she sort of liked Obie.

"Go away, Emil," Amelia said.

Emil just grinned. He didn't seem mad. And he went back to his own desk.

When he was gone, Amelia dug inside her desk.

Katie watched her, feeling sad and worried. She had nothing for show-and-tell. She couldn't show Koala. She'd already done that. She couldn't show the same thing two times. People would laugh.

Amelia was taking a bag out of her desk. She opened it up. She took something out.

It was round and fuzzy and funny-looking. It looked like a fuzzy ball with a face painted on it. It had hair made out of grass. It had two eyes painted on it. And the painted mouth looked like a lady's mouth with lipstick.

"It's a coconut!" Amelia said, holding it up. "See? A real coconut with a face painted on. And know what else?"

"What?" Katie said.

"It has milk inside," Amelia said.

"Does not," Katie said.

"Does too," Amelia said. She held the coconut up to her ear. She shook it. "I can hear it swishing around in there," she said.

She held it out to Katie. "You listen," she said.

Katie took the coconut. She held it up

to her ear. She shook it a little. She didn't hear anything.

She shook it some more.

She still didn't hear anything.

She handed it back to Amelia. "I don't hear anything," she said.

Amelia made a mad face. "How come?" she said. Her voice sounded kind of mad, too. "I can hear it," she said. And she held it up to her ear again.

"Well, maybe I heard a little," Katie said.

"Oh," Amelia said.

"All right, boys and girls!" Mrs. Henry said. "Time to put away your things and stand for the pledge. And then we'll do our show-and-tell."

Katie and Amelia stood up. Everyone else did, too.

"Can you all stand straight and tall?" Mrs. Henry said.

She smiled at the class. Mrs. Henry was always smiling. Katie liked Mrs. Henry. She wanted Mrs. Henry to like her, too. So Katie stood up very straight and tall.

Katie looked across the room at Obie.

He was standing really tall. He already had his hand over his heart. Obie liked this part, the pledge. He said it very loud.

Katie smiled at Obie.

And just then the door opened. It was Tiffany Bianca. She was carrying a big cage, a cage covered with a big white towel.

"I know I'm late, Mrs. Henry," Tiffany said really, really loudly. "But my mother couldn't find a parking space up close with all the buses and I had to be dropped off real close because of Fluffy and . . ."

"It's all right," Mrs. Henry said. She nodded at Tiffany. "Just hang up your coat. Put the cage down here."

"Is it a rabbit?" Emil Marks called out. "Can we see?"

"It's Fluffy!" Tiffany said. "I brought Fluffy. The prettiest rabbit in the whole world."

16

She lifted the cover off the cage, and right away, everybody came up and crowded around. And Tiffany was right. It was the prettiest bunny in the whole wide world. It was a beautiful bunny. A bunny Katie wanted to hold, to touch, to pet. She wanted it so, so much.

And she knew Tiffany wouldn't let her.

Show-and-tell

When they finished the pledge and sat down, Mrs. Henry began taking attendance. While she did, Katie dug through her desk looking for something to show for show-and-tell.

She pulled out some crayons. They were mostly broken and the paper was peeled off. The silver crayon, her favorite, was all worn down.

Boring.

She pulled out a barrette with hair stuck in it.

Yucky.

She found a small rubber ball from her jacks.

Not special enough.

She found an old, wrinkled-up leaf book she had made last fall. She smoothed it out. Most of the leaves were crumpled up.

Nothing. Nothing at all to show.

She looked over at Tiffany with her beautiful white rabbit. What could possibly be as good as a big white rabbit? Tiffany's desk was right next to Katie's, and Tiffany had put the cage on the floor between their desks. Tiffany was bending over, patting the rabbit, her fingers stuck between the cage wires. Fluffy was looking up at Tiffany and nibbling on her fingers. Tiffany was smiling.

Katie bent over, too. She would sneak a touch. Just one.

Very carefully, she put her fingers through the wire cage. Very gently, she patted the fur on Fluffy's back. It was super soft.

20

"Don't touch him!" Tiffany said. "He doesn't like that."

"You're touching him," Katie said back.

"He's my rabbit," Tiffany said.

"Girls?" Mrs. Henry said. "Inside voices, remember?"

"Katie's bothering my rabbit," Tiffany said.

Mrs. Henry didn't answer. She went on with attendance and then lunch tickets.

Katie made a witch face at Tiffany. "I wasn't bothering him," she said. She made her voice an inside voice, but she made it mean, too.

"You were too!" Tiffany said.

"I was just touching his fur," Katie said. "He likes that."

"He hates it," Tiffany said. "He just likes me to touch him."

She pulled the cage closer to her desk.

Katie sat up. She glared at Tiffany. Then she looked down at Fluffy again.

"Stop staring at him," Tiffany said.

"I can look if I want," Katie said.

"Fluffy doesn't like to be stared at," Tiffany said.

She put the cover over Fluffy's cage, closing him up inside.

Katie made another witch face at Tiffany. She was sick of Tiffany. And she felt sorry for Fluffy having to live with Tiffany. She thought it would be awful to have to do that. And then she wondered about what Obie said before — how a bunny might miss his other bunnies. She wondered about that. She wondered if Fluffy had brothers or sisters and if he missed them.

Katie sighed. She still had nothing for show-and-tell.

Katie looked over at Obie. She knew what he had brought for show-and-tell — his sticker collection. He had zillions of airplanes in his sticker collection. Obie loved airplanes, and was always drawing them and making paper airplanes. Grandpa had

22

sent Obie a bunch of new stickers just yesterday.

Katie looked at her friend Amelia. Amelia had that great coconut face to show, even if Katie didn't really believe there was milk inside.

Katie looked at Tiffany again. She wished Tiffany would get in trouble. Katie wouldn't mind that at all. She wondered why Mrs. Henry didn't get mad at Tiffany for being late? When Katie and Obie were late once, they had no recess. And once, Katie had to sit in the time-out chair for being really, really late.

Some things weren't fair.

And then Mrs. Henry was finished with attendance and lunch tickets, and she began show-and-tell.

Mrs. Henry picked Emil first. He went up to the front and took something out of his pocket.

He held it in the palm of his hand, his fingers closed around it. "I have a yo-yo!" he said. "And I can do the best things with it."

He opened his hand and held up the yo-yo. It was bright neon yellow and shiny. He held the string, then let the yo-yo drop from his hand. He brought it back up again. He spun it around, then snapped it up to his hand again. He was very, very good at yo-yo-ing.

"Wow!" Obie said. "That's good."

"I can do that," Tiffany said. "My mother bought me a shiny yo-yo. It's tri-color and . . ."

"I think we're forgetting something," Mrs. Henry said.

Katie knew what they were forgetting. They were forgetting to raise their hands. Katie put her fingers over her mouth. Mrs. Henry smiled at Katie.

Katie never called out without raising her hand. Well, hardly ever.

"What are they forgetting, Katie?" Mrs. Henry asked.

"To raise their hands," Katie answered.

24

"Right," Mrs. Henry said. "Very good." She smiled at Katie.

Katie felt happy.

Mrs. Henry turned back to Emil. "You did very well," she said. "Now, how about letting Arthur go next."

Arthur was Obie's best friend. He went up to the front. He held out his hand. There was a bean in the palm of his hand. It looked like a super-big jelly bean. When he wiggled the bean, it jumped. "It has invisible bugs inside," Arthur said. "That's why it jumps like that."

"Does not," Tawana said.

Tawana was the new girl in class. She was so shy she never spoke up loud. She was so shy, she wouldn't even do show-and-tell. She hardly even spoke on the playground.

Everybody looked at her.

Tawana's face got very red, but she spoke clearly. "They used to have invisible bugs in them," she said. "But now they just use beans inside. The beans roll around. That's why they jump. And that's all."

She clamped her mouth shut.

Mrs. Henry was smiling at Tawana. Katie thought it was because Mrs. Henry was so happy to have Tawana finally say something.

Katie began smiling, too. Because Tawana — Tawana and Arthur — had given Katie an idea. They talked about invisible bugs. Invisible. Something invisible.

Well, Katie had something invisible, too. She had an invisible friend. Her friend's name was Hannah. Hannah lived behind Katie's bed in a town called Hurn-in, Turn-in.

Obie had an invisible friend, too. His friend's name was Jackie. He lived in a town called Vetchen. Vetchen was behind Obie's bed.

Jackie and Hannah were best friends. Katie and Obie didn't play invisible friends anymore. Not much, anyway, now that they were older.

But it would be a good show-and-tell. Nobody had told about invisible friends before. Katie would tell about her invisible friend, Hannah.

She leaned back in her chair. She looked at Tiffany.

Yes. An invisible friend was better than any old rabbit any day.

Katie looked down at Fluffy. She sighed. Well, maybe not really better than this rabbit, this soft, fluffy rabbit. But it was better than nothing. And then she had a funny thought. Actually, she thought, an invisible friend WAS nothing!

She began to smile. She couldn't wait for her turn for show-and-tell.

4

The Invisible Friend

Mrs. Henry didn't pick Katie until the very last, after everyone else had finished their show-and-tell. Mrs. Henry always said that SOMEONE had to be last, and SOMEONE had to be first, and she tried to be fair and give turns. But sometimes Katie felt she got to be last an awful lot of the time.

Finally, though, it was Katie's turn to go, right after blucky, yucky show-off Tiffany. Tiffany wouldn't let anyone pet

Fluffy because she said it would upset him too much.

But Tiffany got to take him out of the cage and hold him for everyone to see.

Katie couldn't help feeling jealous. She couldn't help wishing she could hold Fluffy, too. Just one time. Tiffany was just too mean.

When it was Katie's turn at last, she went up to the front. She stood straight and tall, the way she did when they said the pledge.

"I have something special to show," Katie said.

She took a deep breath.

She looked at Obie.

Obie was looking back at Katie, worried-looking. Katie thought she knew why — he was worried because Katie didn't have that little brown bunny.

Katie smiled at Obie. She didn't mind not having that bunny. Well, she only minded a little bit. She had her invisible friend, Hannah, to talk about. She took another deep breath. She looked out at the class.

And then she had a scary thought, a super-scary thought. What if everybody laughed at her? What if they all thought it was silly to have an invisible friend? Only little kids had invisible friends. Even she and Obie didn't play invisible friends much anymore.

Everyone was looking at her. Mrs. Henry had her eyebrows up, her waiting kind of look.

Katie swallowed. It was kind of hard to breathe. She spoke very fast. "I have a friend," Katie said. "Her name is Hannah. She's my invisible friend. She's fun to be with."

"Hey!" Emil called out. "I had an invisible friend once."

"I used to have an invisible friend," Margaret Anne said.

"I still have one," Arthur said.

"My friend's name is Missy," Margaret Anne said.

"No such thing as invisible," Tiffany called out.

Mrs. Henry put up her hand, two fingers up. Other people put their hands up, two fingers up. It was the signal to hush.

"I think we are all forgetting something this morning," Mrs. Henry said. She smiled at Katie. "Go on, Katie. Tell us more."

Katie smiled. Other people had invisible friends, too! But Tiffany was making a face at her. And Susan was giggling behind her hand. But nobody else was laughing. They knew about invisible friends. And Mrs. Henry wanted to know more. Katie felt much happier. She could even breathe easier.

"Well," Katie said, "her name is Hannah and she's very, very nice. She's smart and she's funny and she can do lots of good stuff. She never gets in trouble. She's good at reading and, and . . ."

Katie stopped. She thought. And then she said, "She's very good at spelling."

Katie was not very good at spelling.

Katie thought some more. "And Hannah has a best friend," Katie went on. She looked over at Obie. "Her best friend's name is Jackie," Katie said.

She didn't say anything about Jackie being Obie's invisible friend, though. She wasn't sure Obie wanted anyone to know about that.

Lots of kids had their hands up, waving, like they wanted to talk about their invisible friends. Margaret Anne was almost falling out of her seat, she was waving so hard.

But Mrs. Henry did that sign with her hand, palm down, like she was patting something invisible — the sign that said, hands down. She looked at Katie again.

"Anything more, Katie?" Mrs. Henry said.

Katie looked all around the room again.

She was happy that nobody was laughing at her. Other people had invisible friends, too!

Then she looked at Tiffany. Tiffany wasn't laughing. She was smiling, though, that mean kind of smile like she did sometimes.

"Just one thing," Katie said. "Hannah hates rabbits. Especially white rabbits."

And then Katie went and sat down.

"Well," Mrs. Henry said. "It seems as if lots of people have had invisible friends. Maybe we'll talk about them all later. For now, let's clear our desks for our spelling test. And afterward, we'll talk about making greeting cards for Easter."

Katie sighed. She hated spelling. But she loved making cards. She was good with glitter and glue. Not so good with drawing, though.

She looked over at Tiffany. Tiffany was a perfect speller. Perfect at drawing, too.

"No such thing as invisible," Tiffany said, leaning close to Katie's desk and speaking quietly. "Only babies have invisible friends."

"You're invisible," Katie said. She smiled a mean smile, just like Tiffany had done.

"I am not!" Tiffany said.

"Are too," Katie said. She pretended to be looking all around. "Where are you?" she said. "I can hear you, but I can't see you. You must be invisible now."

"Stop it!" Tiffany said. She sounded like she was about to cry. "I am not invisible!"

Mrs. Henry looked up, frowning. "What's going on, girls?" she said.

"Mrs. Henry!" Tiffany said. "Katie's being mean. She said I was invisible."

"Katie!" Mrs. Henry said. "Is that true?"

Katie didn't answer. She didn't look at Mrs. Henry, either.

"Katie!" Mrs. Henry said again. "Did you just say something to tease Tiffany?"

Katie looked down at her desk. She still didn't answer. She wished she really could be invisible.

"Katie!" Mrs. Henry said. "I'm speaking to you."

Katie took a big breath. She looked at Tiffany. She looked at Tiffany's rabbit. She looked at Mrs. Henry.

Mrs. Henry wasn't smiling at her.

Katie looked down at her desk. "No," she said very quietly.

"No?" Mrs. Henry said.

"No," Katie said. "I didn't say anything bad."

"Then who did?" Mrs. Henry said.

Katie took a deep breath. She didn't look at Mrs. Henry. But she said, "Maybe Hannah did."

5

The Earth Digger

Katie was glad when the day was finally over. It hadn't been a good day. She had a note from Mrs. Henry to give to Mom about her not-so-good behavior. Katie had had to sit in the time-out chair two times. First time, it was because of calling Tiffany the name, invisible. And later that day, Katie had another time-out because she had pushed in line.

Katie hadn't meant to push. It was just that she was in a hurry for recess. And she couldn't help it if Susan fell down when she got pushed. Susan wasn't fat enough was her trouble. She should eat more, and then she'd get fat like Rebecca and she couldn't get pushed down.

Katie was glad when she and Obie got off the bus and were finally home.

But right outside the house, they both stopped short.

There were two men working in the yard. They had a big earthmover there. One was sitting high up in the earthmover, making it go. It was digging deep holes in the yard. Big, big holes.

The other man was yelling directions at him, showing him where to dig.

Katie and Obie both stood and stared.

"What are they doing?" Obie said.

"Making a mess!" Katie said.

She looked at the men. The one yelling directions was very big and tall and he had a big beard. He looked sort of like a Viking who Katie had read about in a book. The driving man was smaller but he had a very fat stomach. They both had on orange vests.

They stopped their machine when Katie and Obie came into the yard.

"Hey!" Katie said to them. "Why are you messing up our yard?"

The big man smiled at her. "We're not really messing it up," he said.

Katie frowned at him. "You are too," she said. "Does my dad know you're doing this?"

He laughed. "Your father hired us," he said.

"For what?" Obie said.

"To cut down the sick trees and put in new ones," the man said.

"Trees get sick?" Katie said.

"Sure," the man said. He pointed. "Look at that one."

It was a tall tree with white bark on it. It was bent over, its branches almost touching the ground. It did look kind of tired.

"Did you see any rabbits when you dug?" Katie asked.

"Lots of them," the man said. "There must be a whole rabbit family in this yard. Now out of here, you two. We need to dig just one more hole before we call it quits for the day. We'll be back tomorrow to put in the new trees and get rid of the old."

Katie and Obie backed up to the fence.

The earthmover started digging again.

"Know what, Obie?" Katie said. She leaned close to Obie because it was hard to be heard over the earth digger. "We could build a fort down in one of those holes. And make a trap to catch a rabbit down there."

Obie didn't answer.

He was staring at the earth digger as it started digging another hole. The digger had big prongs like teeth. It grabbed big mouthfuls of earth and tossed them aside.

"Wow!" Obie said. He looked at Katie

and sighed. "Wouldn't you love to work that thing? Or take a ride on it?"

"No," Katie said.

"I would," Obie said.

"So ask them if they'll let you," Katie said.

Obie shook his head.

Katie made a frowny face. "How come?" she said.

Obie didn't answer.

Katie started to say, baby. But she didn't. She knew Obie was shy sometimes.

When the earth digger stopped, Katie moved away from the fence. "Hey, mister!" she yelled. "Can my brother ride on your digging thing?"

The man looked down at Obie. He looked at Katie.

He looked at the other man.

They both shrugged.

"Sure," the driver man said. "You can both come up here."

"Okay!" Katie yelled.

She and Obie both ran for the big machine.

But just then Mom appeared at the kitchen door. She had Baby-Child on one hip the way she almost always did. "Come on in, Katie, Obie," Mom called, leaning out the door. "I don't want you bothering the men."

"We're not bothering them, Mom," Obie said.

"Yes, you are," Mom said. "Now come on in."

"Just one minute, Mom?" Katie said.

"Not even one," Mom said. "It's not safe out there."

Katie looked at Obie. He looked so sad.

She looked up at the men.

The man in the earthmover was taking off his vest.

The other one was locking up his toolbox.

Katie looked up at Mom in the doorway. Baby-Child began to yell. Baby-Child was always yelling. If you put Baby-Child down, he yelled. If you stopped walking him around, he yelled. If you didn't feed him what he wanted, when he wanted, he yelled. He could get a gold star at yelling.

Now he was yelling so loud that Katie couldn't hear what Mom was saying. But she knew it even if she couldn't hear. Mom was waving to Katie and Obie — a come-on-in-this-minute kind of wave.

Katie looked at Obie again.

He looked really, really sad.

"Don't worry," Katie said quickly. "Tomorrow morning. Just like this morning. Only better. We'll come out early and catch a rabbit. And ride the machine all by ourselves. You wait and see."

6

The World's Fluffiest Bunny

But next morning, Obie didn't get to go out on the earth digger and Katie didn't get to catch a bunny. Because when they tiptoed downstairs, Dad was already up. He was sitting at the kitchen table, reading his paper and drinking coffee. And it was snowing out! It was April, but it was snowing. So Dad said, no outside, no way, not this early and not in the snow.

When it was finally time to go to school, the snow had turned to rain. And Katie felt a little worried in her stomach.

The note. She had forgotten to give Mom the note from Mrs. Henry. Well, she hadn't exactly forgotten. But she knew Mom would scold at least a little bit. And Katie didn't feel like getting scolded.

So she kind of accidentally forgot the note.

When she got to school, she didn't look at Mrs. Henry. She tried to hide a little bit. She slid down in her seat so she was hidden behind Rebecca, who sat in front of her. Rebecca was a new girl. She was the tallest and the fattest girl in class. She had a big head and fat, red ears. Rebecca's family moved a lot, and Rebecca had gone to five different schools last year. This year, she had been left back because she couldn't catch up on the work because of moving around so much. Katie thought it would be awful to be left back.

Katie hid behind Rebecca's fat head and fat ears.

All morning, Katie stayed sort of hidden. She stood right behind Rebecca during the pledge. She sat right behind Rebecca during the lunch count. And she said, "Here," but she didn't look at Mrs. Henry during the attendance.

Katie thought that maybe Mrs. Henry wouldn't notice her at all. And that way, she'd forget all about the note.

It seemed to work, too. Mrs. Henry didn't even ask about the note. Katie thought it was because Mrs. Henry was excited. Mrs. Henry said she had big plans for spring. After attendance, they were going to start their Easter project.

"Now, boys and girls," Mrs. Henry said when they were all settled in their places and all the morning chores were done. "I have some good plans for you. We're going to make special Easter cards for your grandparents today. And if you have no grandparent, you can make a card for your special grown-up friend."

She smiled at the class.

Katie knew why Mrs. Henry said "special friends." It was because some kids didn't have a grandma or grandpa living anywhere. Katie thought it would be very sad to have no grandma or grandpa.

"Now," Mrs. Henry said, "I want you to think about what you love about your special person, and write it down. I think Easter and spring are fine times to tell them how special they are to us."

Right away, people's hands went shooting up.

Katie forgot that she was hiding, and she stuck her hand up, too. She had four grandparents. She wanted to know if she could make cards for each one.

Emil put up his hand, but he didn't wait for Mrs. Henry to call on him. He just called out. Emil always called out. He forgot.

"I don't have Easter, Mrs. Henry!" he called out.

Mrs. Henry just looked at him. Her eyebrows were up. "What did you forget, Emil?" Mrs. Henry said.

Emil frowned. He looked all around. "I don't know," he said.

"He forgot to raise his hand," Tiffany called out.

"And you forgot to raise yours!" Katie said.

"Now, girls," Mrs. Henry said.

She frowned at Katie, and Katie quick looked away. She shouldn't have made Mrs. Henry notice her.

Mrs. Henry looked back at Emil.

Emil put one hand over his mouth. He raised the other hand.

"Yes, Emil?" Mrs. Henry said.

She said it in a nice way. Mrs. Henry was always nice to Emil. Well, she was nice to everybody. Most of the time.

"I don't have Easter," Emil said. "I have Passover in spring."

"That's right," Mrs. Henry said. She smiled at Emil. "But we can all celebrate spring, right? So you can make a special spring card for your grandmother."

"It could be a Passover card," Emil said.

"It could be," Mrs. Henry said.

Katie knew Emil didn't celebrate Easter. He didn't celebrate Christmas, either. He had Passover and Hanukkah instead.

Katie thought Passover sounded neat. Emil said once that they ate lots and lots and lots of food at Passover. And they made a place at the table for someone who didn't come. His name was Elijah. Every year they waited for him, and they opened the door looking for him, but he never showed up.

Katie thought Elijah sounded sort of like an invisible friend. Katie thought it would be neat if Elijah really did show up some day.

"So, boys and girls," Mrs. Henry said. "You can make several cards, one for each of your grandparents or special friends. There's glue and paper and colored pencils and ribbons up here on the art table. You can make any decorations you want on the outside. Inside, we'll put these words."

Mrs. Henry turned around to the blackboard. She wrote out these words. She used her prettiest script writing. It said:

You are special to me.

You do these special things. . . .

Mrs. Henry turned back to the class. She smiled. "And then you can list what they do that's special," she said.

Right away, Katie started to think. Her grandmas and grandpa did all sorts of special things. Grandpa always brought her presents and he knew when she was scared or felt bad and he always made it better. Grandma gave her special sleep-overs with her and Great-grandma — girl nights, she called them. Katie had lots of special things to put on her cards.

"Now, you can come up in rows to the art table," Mrs. Henry said. "Come take your supplies. One row at a time."

She pointed to Katie's row first.

Katie was glad to go first for a

change. When she went up with her row, she walked close behind Rebecca.

There was beautiful stuff on the art table. There were lace and ribbons and cotton balls and glue and scissors and cutouts of bunnies.

Katie picked out a pink piece of construction paper for the card. She picked up some cotton balls. Cotton balls! She could make a cotton-ball bunny on her card a cotton-ball body and a cotton-ball head. She picked up pink construction paper for the ears. But then she thought pink ears wouldn't show up on pink paper. So she put back one piece of pink paper and picked up yellow paper instead. She picked up glue and scissors and some sparkles.

Katie loved sparkles.

"We're waiting, Katie," Mrs. Henry said.

Katie looked around. Everybody else in her row was finished. Rebecca was gone.

Katie hurried back to her seat.

Amelia's row got to go next.

Back at her desk, Katie started laying out her supplies. She put the cotton balls on the paper, one on top, one on bottom. She held it out, looking at it. Would it look like a bunny?

Tiffany was stretching out her neck, looking to see what Katie was doing.

Katie covered her card with her hand. She started humming quietly. "Bunny, bunny, bunny," Katie hummed. "I'm making a bunny. The fluffiest bunny in the world."

Tiffany didn't say anything.

Katie went right on humming. "Bunny, bunny, bunny," she hummed. "World's fluffiest bunny."

Tiffany leaned closer. "That's a good idea," she said.

Katie looked at Tiffany. Katie's eyebrows went up.

"Making a cotton bunny, I mean," Tiffany said. "That's a good idea."

"Oh," Katie said.

She bent over her card again. She

added another cotton ball to the bunny's middle to make him fatter. She sat back and looked at him. She smiled and took a deep breath. She felt a little happier then. She had nice stuff to make a nice bunny. Tiffany had said something nice. And Mrs. Henry had forgotten all about the note. Katie thought maybe it was going to be a pretty good day.

Katie thought of Daddy then. Daddy was always saying how each Saturday was a practically perfect day. Katie thought that today would be a practically perfect day if she only had a really real bunny of her own.

And then Katie began to smile. Because she had a thought. Tomorrow was Saturday. And she thought she knew how to have a perfectly perfect day. And how to get a perfectly perfect bunny for her very own.

7

A Special Treat

Next day was Saturday, Katie's best day of the week. It was the day she got to do something alone with Daddy. They always started with breakfast out, and then they went to the grocery store. Katie got to pick out the cereal for the week and sometimes the cookies. Then, when they finished shopping, Daddy took Katie for a special treat, just for her.

This Saturday, Katie had come up with a wonderful idea for her special treat. She had been thinking about it since the day before — a plan about a bunny. If only Daddy would say yes. Katie thought maybe she had to be extra good to get this extra-special treat, though.

Katie was dressed and ready, playing with her Beanie Babies when Daddy came down the next morning.

"Hey, Toots!" Daddy said. He came over and kissed her forehead. "Where to today?"

It was their little private joke. Daddy always said that, and Katie always said, "McDonald's," and Daddy always took her there. Just once, he didn't, though. That was the time he made her go to the diner for oatmeal because he said it was better for them. Katie hated that time.

"How about McDonald's?" Katie said. And then she said, "Or we could get oatmeal at the diner if you want."

Daddy put his eyebrows up. "Really?" he said.

Katie took a big breath. "If you want," she said.

Daddy made a thinking kind of face. "Well," he said. "I think McDonald's would be all right this time."

Katie let out her breath. She smiled. "I think so, too," she said.

When they went outside to the car, they stopped to look at the holes in the yard. The men hadn't come back with the trees because it had been raining and snowing too much the day before. Now the holes were filled with water and mud.

Katie liked muddy holes. She bent over and looked hard at the mud. She was looking for bunny tracks. She didn't see any.

"What a mess," Daddy said.

"I like it," Katie said.

Daddy laughed and helped Katie get in the car and get her seat belt on. Katie had to sit in back. Air bags were the reason. Kids couldn't sit in front if there were air bags.

Katie thought there were all kinds of

bad rules for kids. But she wouldn't complain. Not today.

They got to McDonald's and were starting on hotcakes, when Katie thought it would be good to begin.

"Daddy?" she said. "What do you think about bunnies?"

"Oh," Daddy said. "I think bunnies are very sweet. Don't you?"

Katie nodded. She smiled. "Yes," she said. "I think they're very, very sweet."

She ate some more bites of hotcakes. "Know what?" she said. "I think white bunnies are the best. And brown bunnies are second best."

"Brown bunnies are wild bunnies, I think," Daddy said.

Katie nodded. "They are," she said. "White bunnies come in cages."

She looked at Daddy.

But Daddy wasn't looking back. He was frowning down at the shopping list in his hand. "Looks like we're out of everything today," he said. "We'd better hustle to get to the store."

"Daddy?" Katie said. "I wish I had a white bunny."

Daddy nodded, but he didn't look up from his list.

"Tiffany has a white bunny in a cage," Katie said. "It's very, very sweet. And it's no trouble at all."

"That's nice," Daddy said.

"Daddy?" Katie said. She took a big breath. "Could I have a bunny, you think?"

Daddy looked up. He smiled at Katie. He reached out and ruffled her hair. "No, Toots," he said. "No bunny."

"But why?" Katie said. "I really want one! Why can't I?"

"Because," Daddy said.

"Because why?" Katie said.

"Because they're too much trouble, Katie," Daddy said. "Remember how your school bunny got sick and died? They get diseases. They make messes if you let them out of the cage. They're just far too much trouble. So no, no bunny."

"Tiffany's rabbit doesn't make any messes," Katie said. "And it doesn't get sick." Then she said the rest very, very fast. "And besides, I'll take care of it all by myself. I promise, Daddy, honest. You won't have to do anything with it. I won't let it get sick. And you know how you always take me out for a special treat on Saturday? That's the treat I want today. I won't ask for anything anymore, not next week, not ever. Just this once? Please?"

She folded her hands like she was begging.

Daddy smiled. He reached out and ruffled Katie's hair again. But again he said, "I'm sorry, Toots. The answer is no."

"But, Daddy!" Katie said. "Please? I have to have something to hold, something to pet."

Daddy laughed. "Pet your Beanie Babies," he said.

"It's not the same!" Katie said. She made a mad face at him.

Daddy sighed. "Look, Katie," he said. "Finish up your breakfast. You ready to go shopping?"

"No," Katie said.

"We have to get Easter egg coloring," Daddy said.

"So?" Katie said. She folded her arms. "I don't want Easter egg coloring. I want a bunny."

"Look, Katie," Daddy said. He used his I'm-almost-mad voice. "We are not getting you a rabbit. And that's all there is to it."

Katie made squinty-eyes at Daddy. She hated it when he said, that's all there is to it. Her brothers Sam and Matt said that to her, too. But they said it like this: That's tuit!

"That's not tuit," Katie said, and she used her I-am-mad voice. "That's the only treat I want. So there!"

Daddy took a big, deep breath. He let it out through his nose with a big sound.

Katie knew what that meant. It meant he was going to get mad. It was the same thing Mrs. Henry did before she got mad.

So what? Katie could do that, too.

She took a deep, slow breath, deep and mad, just like Daddy and just like Mrs. Henry. Then she looked up at the ceiling just like Mrs. Henry did sometimes. And she said what Mrs. Henry said sometimes. "You are impossible," she said.

"That's not appropriate language, Toots," Daddy said. But he sounded like he wanted to laugh.

Katie quick looked at him.

"Come on," he said. He smiled at her, and reached out a hand. "Let's be friends?"

"If I get a bunny," Katie said.

"What you're getting is a trip back home if you don't stop this," Daddy said. "One of your brothers can come shopping with me instead."

Katie felt water come to her eyes.

Daddy stood up and reached for her hand.

Katie stood up, too. She let Daddy take her hand while they went to the car. But she thought mean thoughts at him. He wouldn't even listen. He didn't understand how she needed something to pet, something real. Not just Beanie Babies.

In the car, in the rearview mirror, Katie could see that Daddy was smiling at her. She didn't smile back at him. Instead, she looked away. She talked to Hannah inside her head. And she told Hannah all the mean things she was thinking about Daddy.

8

The Secret

That night, when the whole family was in the family room watching a video about Dalmatians, Katie went upstairs. Very quietly, she tiptoed into Mom and Dad's room. She had a plan. She'd thought and thought about this. She knew just what to do.

She went over to the bedside table and picked up the phone. She dialed a number that she knew by heart. It was the number of Grandma and Great-grandma. They lived together in a big house across town. They came to visit on Sundays some-times. Some other times, Katie spent an overnight with them.

Grandma and Great-grandma were two of Katie's best friends. Her other grandma and grandpa were her other best friends. Grandpa was always bringing pres-ents for Katie and her brothers. But that grandpa and grandma lived kind of far away. Katie thought it would be best to try the closest ones first.

She listened while the phone rang. It rang and rang. Katie counted the rings. Twelve. Thirteen. Fourteen. After it rang fifteen times, Katie hung up. Even though Great-grandma couldn't hear too well sometimes, Katie knew she'd hear fifteen phone rings.

Well, she'd just try Grandma and Grandpa. She hoped it would be Grandpa who would answer.

She dialed their number. She knew that number by heart, too. While she waited for it to ring, she flopped down across Mom and Daddy's bed, her head in the pile of pillows.

The phone rang just two times when Grandpa picked it up.

"Hi, Grandpa!" Katie said.

"Katie, my dear!" Grandpa said.

Katie began to smile. She could just picture Grandpa, standing there with the phone. She knew he was smiling. She could hear it in his voice. And she knew he was smiling at her.

"How's my girl?" Grandpa said.

"I'm fine," Katie said. "How are you?"

"Why, I'm just terrific!" Grandpa said. "Guess what I did today?"

Katie tried to imagine. Grandpa was always doing all sorts of good stuff. He ran marathon races and regular races. He raced cars sometimes in road rallies. And one time he went parasailing. That's when you sail up in the air on a kind of parachute behind a boat.

Katie couldn't think what fun thing he'd done today. So she just said, "What?"

"I went skydiving!" he said. "I jumped out of a plane in a parachute."

"Wow!" Katie said. "Were you scared?"

"Terrified," Grandpa said. "But you know what, Katie?" He made his voice very low and quiet. "I didn't tell your grandma I was scared."

"I won't tell," Katie said.

Grandpa laughed. "I know you won't," he said. "That will be our secret. And want to know what else?"

"What else?" Katie said.

"Tomorrow I'm going to do it again," Grandpa said. "Five of us are jumping together."

Katie smiled. She pictured herself being one of five people jumping out of a plane in a parachute. "I wish I could do that with you," she said.

"Maybe you will someday," Grandpa said. "Maybe I'll buy you lessons someday."

"You will?" Katie said. "Really?"

"When you're bigger," Grandpa said.

"Not now. I don't think your mom or dad would like that."

"I know," Katie said. "They get scared of little things like that."

"So what's new, Katie?" Grandpa said. "Easter's coming. What do you want in your Easter basket?"

Katie smiled. Exactly what she hoped he'd ask. She took a big breath. "A bunny," she said.

Grandpa laughed. "A bunny?!" he said. "The Easter bunny brings the basket. I don't think he gets IN the basket."

"I know that!" Katie said. "I don't want the Easter bunny! I want a real bunny."

"You do?" Grandpa said.

Katie nodded.

"Katie?" Grandpa said.

"Oh," Katie said. She forgot sometimes that people couldn't see her nod on the phone. "Yes," she said. "I want a real bunny. For a pet."

"Know what?" Grandpa said. "I always wanted a bunny when I was a child. Is that what Mom and Dad are getting for you? Or is that what you'd like me to get you?"

"I want you to get it for me," Katie said.

"Well, I could probably do that," Grandpa said. "I'd love to do that. If that's what you want."

"I do want it!" Katie said. "I really, really do."

"Well," Grandpa said. "Then that's settled!"

"But know something?" Katie said. She hated to ask for too much, but she knew she had to ask this. "I'd need other stuff, too," she said. "Like a cage and some bunny food and sleeping straw and stuff. Is that too much?"

Grandpa laughed. "Of course it's not too much. I wouldn't get you a bunny without all the necessary bunny equipment."

Katie smiled. "Oh, good," she said. "Grandpa? You think bunnies get lonely?

Without their brothers or mom and dad, I mean?"

Grandpa laughed. "I don't think we can get you more than one bunny, Katie," he said.

"I know that!" Katie said. "I just wondered."

"I don't think they get lonely," Grandpa said. "Not if they have a little girl like you to play with."

Katie took a big breath. That was just what she had hoped he'd say.

Grandpa didn't say anything for a minute. Katie could hear some funny, puffy sounds. She knew what he was doing. He was puffing on his pipe.

After a minute, he said, "A real live bunny. What do your mom and dad have to say about that?"

For a minute, Katie didn't answer. She could feel a funny, sickly feeling coming in her stomach. Her heart was bumping very, very fast.

"Katie?" Grandpa said.

Katie didn't want to lie. She thought very fast. "Oh," she said. "I think it will be okay with them. I mean, with Mom. I mean, Mom didn't say no."

"Oh," Grandpa said. "Then I guess that's all right. And I'm going to see you before Easter, too. I'm running a race in your town the week before Easter."

"Oh," Katie said. "But don't bring the bunny till Easter, okay?"

"Of course not!" Grandpa said. "It's an Easter present."

Katie took a big breath. "Grandpa?" she said. "Let's keep it a secret for a while, okay? You know how we're keeping a secret from Grandma?"

"We are?" Grandpa said.

"Yes!" Katie said. "Remember? We're keeping a secret about you being scared?"

"Oh!" Grandpa said. "I almost forgot. Yes."

"Let's keep this a secret, too," Katie said. "Just for a while. Okay?"

"Okay," Grandpa said. "You let me know when I can tell."

"I will," Katie said.

And she would. She would tell him when it was okay. She would tell everyone she was getting a bunny. She'd even tell Daddy. She just wasn't sure when that would be.

9

A Melting Snowflake

On Monday at school, everyone had time to work on their Easter cards before they went to the big assembly. The assembly was for Author's Day. An author was coming to their school to talk to them about books and writing.

The author's name was Amanda Pickle. She was going to autograph the books the children had bought at the book fair. She had written a whole lot of books about bunnies and owls. Katie's class had read one of the author's books. It was called

Rabbit Days. It was about a bunny who ran away from home on Easter morning and ended up living with a real family of real people. The bunny didn't like carrots but it liked hard-boiled eggs, Easter eggs.

Everybody thought it was a fun book because it was silly and it had a happy ending. And best of all, the author wrote that it was a true story! Everybody had a whole lot of questions to ask the author. They had written down their questions.

Katie had questions, too, important ones. Now that she was getting her own bunny, she wanted to know all about Mrs. Pickle's real live bunny. She wanted to know if the bunny missed its family. She especially wanted to know if the bunny liked living with Mrs. Pickle instead of with real bunnies. And she wanted to know if the part about the eggs was true and if Katie should feed eggs to her bunny. She wanted to ask the author those questions and she couldn't wait for question-and-answer time.

When it was time for the assembly, Mrs. Henry lined them up to go. They went to a big room where they ate lunch and had assemblies. At lunch, they sat at tables and called it a cafeteria. At assembly, they sat on the floor and called it a cafetorium.

Now it was a cafetorium.

Katie quickly lined up with her best friend, Amelia, holding hands. In their other hands, they carried books to be signed by the author. Katie had the book *Rabbit Days*.

Amelia had a different book. She'd bought a book about owls. It was called *Owl Night*.

"All right, children," Mrs. Henry said when they all got to the cafetorium. "Sit on the floor, flat on your bottoms, legs crossed, and be very, very quiet. Best behavior."

Katie sat down next to Amelia.

Tiffany sat down on the other side of Katie.

Katie scooted away from Tiffany and closer to Amelia.

The rest of the school was still filing in. There were a lot of kids, but no author, not that Katie could see. There was just a tall lady with big curly hair fixing a speaking system on the stage.

"I wonder if that's the author," Katie said, pointing to the curly-haired lady.

"No," Amelia said. "The author is this lady. Look."

She held out her owl book. The author's picture was on the back of the owl book.

"Oh," Katie said. "I forgot to look there."

Katie looked at the picture then. The author looked kind of old, but kind of nice. She had big hair and a round face and huge round glasses.

"She looks like an owl," Katie said.

Amelia laughed. "Look at this," she said. She made her eyes big and wide at Katie like an owl.

Katie laughed. "Maybe that's why she writes about owls," Katie said.

"She writes about bunnies, too," Amelia said.

"Maybe she looks like a bunny, too," Katie said. "Look."

She pulled up her top lip and let her big teeth stick out over her bottom lip. She thought she looked like Bugs Bunny.

Amelia began to laugh.

"Girls!" Mrs. Henry said.

Katie looked up.

Mrs. Henry was standing at the end of the row, looking at Katie and Amelia. She had her finger on her lips. "Turn front," she said. "And remember — pancakes and snowflakes."

Katie nodded. She knew what that meant. Sit as flat as a pancake and be quiet as a snowflake.

Katie turned to the front. She wondered what it would be like to be a pancake. She thought it would probably be pretty boring. Then she thought it might feel scary to get fried up in a frying pan and eaten.

She didn't think she wanted to be a pancake.

Katie thought about being a snowflake. She wondered how snowflakes felt. Not as bored as pancakes, she thought. Except if you were a snowflake, you would melt after a while.

Katie wondered how it felt to melt.

She closed her eyes and imagined. She scrunched herself down. She tried to feel herself melting.

She opened her eyes. She looked around. Mrs. Henry wasn't looking. She was talking to the other second-grade teacher. Katie poked Amelia.

"Watch this," Katie whispered. "I'm a snowflake and I'm melting."

She scrunched herself down toward the floor. She made herself get lower and lower on the floor. She was a snowflake melting into a puddle.

Amelia giggled.

Katie melted even more. She melted until she was stretched out flat on the floor, looking up at the ceiling. Then she closed her eyes. She felt herself being totally melted. She wasn't even a snowflake anymore. She was just a puddle of water.

Somebody poked Katie. Katie opened her eyes.

It was Amelia. Amelia was pointing to Mrs. Henry.

Mrs. Henry made a come-over-here-to-me signal to Katie.

Katie got up and walked to the end of the row. She looked down at her feet. She knew everyone was looking at her and she could feel her face get hot.

Mrs. Henry pointed to a place on the floor, right by her chair. "Just sit here by me," she said. "I'm very disappointed in you."

Katie sat down. She looked back at her row.

She saw Tiffany slide over closer to Amelia.

She saw Tiffany whisper something to Amelia.

Then she saw Amelia turn and smile at Tiffany.

Katie looked up at Mrs. Henry and made a mad face at her.

Mrs. Henry just shook her head at her. "You forgot," Mrs. Henry said. "Pancake, snowflake."

I didn't forget! Katie thought. I was a snowflake just like you told me.

Only thing was, she didn't say it out loud. She just said it inside her head. Because she had a feeling Mrs. Henry just wouldn't understand.

10

The Author Visit

Just then the author, Mrs. Pickle, came out onstage. Mrs. Rubin, the librarian, came out with her. The author had big hair and big glasses, just like in her picture. She was old like in her picture. But she had a nice smile, like Mrs. Henry had when she wasn't mad. Everybody started to clap.

Some of the big boys made whistling, stamping sounds.

Mrs. Rubin made a frowny face at them.

When everybody got quiet, Mrs. Rubin said, "Boys and girls, this is Mrs. Pickle, our visiting author for the day. She came all the way from Missouri to talk to us. Does anyone know where Missouri is?"

Katie didn't know where Missouri was. She didn't care where Missouri was. She picked at the rubber on her sneakers. It was peeling off. All she cared about was finding out more about rabbits.

Tiffany's hand shot up.

A lot of other people put their hands up, too. Even some of the kindergarten babies put their hands up.

Mrs. Rubin picked one of the kindergarten babies. "Yes, Sabrina?" Mrs. Rubin said.

"I wrote a book once," Sabrina said.

"That's nice," Mrs. Rubin said. "But does anyone know where Missouri is?"

Lots of kids were waving their hands.

Mrs. Rubin picked another kindergarten baby. "Yes, Tracy?" she said. "What do you think?"

"My mother's having a baby," Tracy said.

Mrs. Rubin smiled but it was kind of a fakey smile. "Well, that's nice, too," she said.

She took a deep breath, and looked around the cafetorium again. Katie looked, too.

Tiffany was still waving her hand super-hard. She had gotten up on her knees so she stuck up higher than anyone else. She wasn't supposed to do that.

Katie looked at Mrs. Henry, but Mrs. Henry didn't notice that Tiffany was kneeling up. Mrs. Henry was correcting papers.

Mrs. Rubin saw Tiffany. Mrs. Rubin smiled. All grown-ups always smiled at Tiffany. "Yes, Tiffany?" she said.

Tiffany scrambled to her feet. She stood straight and tall. She said, "Missouri is in the middle part of the country. It's bordered by the Missouri River and it has lots of cows. It's far, far away."

"Very good, Tiffany!" Mrs. Rubin said.

"I'm very proud of you. You may sit down now."

Tiffany sat down. But first she looked all around her. She looked over at Katie and she smiled her mean, show-offy smile.

Katie made a mean smile back.

Mrs. Rubin turned to Mrs. Pickle. "And," Mrs. Rubin said, "Mrs. Pickle lives in the country but she is happy to be here visiting you today. Aren't you, Mrs. Pickle?"

Mrs. Pickle smiled. She nodded, like she was happy to be visiting them.

"So," Mrs. Rubin said. "Without further ado, I'm going to let Mrs. Pickle talk to you all about reading and writing. So sit up straight and tall and listen."

Mrs. Rubin hurried down off the stage.

Katie sat up straight and tall. She was ready to listen. She wanted to know what it was like to live in the country in Missouri. She wanted to know if there were lots of rabbits there. She wanted Mrs. Pickle to tell about that.

But Mrs. Pickle didn't talk at all about rabbits. Mrs. Pickle talked about writing. She talked about ideas. She told about how she got the ideas for her stories. She told about how long it took to write a book. She told how she wrote stories when she was a little girl. She said how all the boys and girls could call themselves authors because if you wrote a story, you were an author, she said.

She talked and talked and talked. But she didn't say one word about her rabbit.

Katie thought Mrs. Pickle was nice, but kind of boring.

But then, at last, Mrs. Pickle stopped talking. She said it was time for the children to talk, for question-and-answer period.

Right away, Katie stuck up her hand.

Oh, please, oh, please, oh, please, pick me! she thought.

But Mrs. Pickle didn't pick her. Mrs. Pickle picked Margaret Anne instead.

"Which of your books is your favorite book?" Margaret Anne asked.

Mrs. Pickle said she couldn't answer that. All of her books were her favorite books. She said it was like asking which of her children was her favorite child in her family. And of course she didn't have a favorite child.

Katie didn't believe Mrs. Pickle didn't have a favorite book. She didn't believe Mrs. Pickle didn't have a favorite child, either. Katie had a favorite child in her family. It was Obie.

Katie had a not-so-favorite child in her family, too. Her not-so-favorite child was Baby-Child.

Mrs. Pickle asked for more questions.

People were waving their hands like crazy.

Katie waved her hand so hard she thought it would fall off.

But Mrs. Pickle still didn't pick her. She picked Emil.

"Are your stories true?" Emil asked.

"Well, some," Mrs. Pickle answered. "But authors make up stories, too. They're not all true. They're fiction."

Katie wondered if that meant authors tell lies. If you were an author, were you allowed to tell lies?

Katie began waving her hand again. She waved it very, very hard.

"Well," Mrs. Pickle said, "I'm afraid there's no more time for questions."

Katie couldn't help herself. She jumped to her feet.

"Oh, please!" she called out. "Please, just one more!"

But Mrs. Pickle was already gathering up her papers. She was getting ready to leave the stage.

Mrs. Henry made a frowny face at Katie. She pointed her finger at the floor.

Katie knew what that meant. It meant sit down.

But Katie couldn't sit down.

"Mrs. Pickle!" she called out. "Please tell about your rabbit."

Mrs. Pickle looked up. "Not much to tell," Mrs. Pickle said. "I told it all in the book. Rabbits really aren't very interesting creatures."

And then she went down from the stage while everyone began clapping.

Mrs. Pickle was coming down the aisle on her way to the autograph table. She passed right by Katie. Up close, she looked even older than she did from far away.

When she passed Katie, she leaned close and smiled. "Really," she said. "Rabbits are very dumb creatures."

"You lie!" Katie said. She meant to say it in a whisper, but it came out kind of loud. "You're old and mean and you lie," she said.

Mrs. Pickle kept going to the autograph table. She didn't seem to hear. But Mrs. Henry heard.

She put a hand on Katie's arm. "All right, missy," she said. She held Katie's arm too tight. "No recess for you today. And time-out chair when we get back to the class."

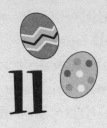

11

Bunnies *Aren't* Dumb

When Katie got home that day, she dropped her backpack in the hall and yelled hi to Mom. Then she went right up to her room. She felt a little sick in her stomach. She had another note from Mrs. Henry to Mom. And this time, Mrs. Henry wasn't going to forget about the note. Katie could tell. Mrs Henry said it was very rude to call anyone a name. She said it was especially rude to say the name of "mean liar" to an adult.

Katie didn't care. She thought Mrs. Pickle did tell lies.

Bunnies weren't dumb at all. They were very fun and very interesting. But Katie was a little worried about being in trouble again.

She was also a little worried about the bunny she was going to get. Easter was coming really soon. And she hadn't said anything to Daddy yet about the bunny Grandpa was getting for her.

She sat on her bed, thinking. She wondered what to do about the note. And she wondered what to do about the bunny.

She went to her window and looked out. It was gray and rainy again. She wondered if wild bunnies ran around in the rain or if they hid in their rabbit holes till the rain stopped. She wondered if brown bunnies played with white bunnies and how white bunnies got to be white and brown ones got to be brown. She wondered what to name her bunny.

She looked out at the tree just outside her window. A squirrel was scampering up the tree chasing after another squirrel. Squirrels were fast, very, very fast. Just like bunnies.

Katie sighed. Bunnies weren't dumb, she knew that. Bunnies were smart and fast and they were very, very sweet. But they did cause trouble. And Katie was in trouble. Again. Big, big trouble.

She went back and sat on her bed. She picked up Big Bear and smoothed the red ribbon around his neck. She held him close.

"I had to sit in the time-out chair today," she whispered to him.

Katie thought she heard Big Bear sigh. She knew that Big Bear felt bad for her.

"Only bad kids have to sit in the time-out chair," Katie told Big Bear.

She lifted Big Bear then and held him close to her face. She thought she heard him say that she wasn't a bad kid.

"I know," she whispered to him. "But I have this dumb note for Mom."

Big Bear nodded. He sighed again.

Out in the hall, Katie could hear her brothers Sam and Matt playing a game. They were yelling, "Dive in!" And then there was a thumpy sound and they went racing down the stairs. In a few minutes, she heard them come racing back up again.

This time, she heard Matt yell, *"Bonzai!"* And she heard all the thumping all over again.

She wondered what they were playing. She was a little lonely. She wondered if they would let her play with them.

She put Big Bear down and opened her door.

Sam and Matt were standing by the stair railing. They had some little toys lined up on the railing.

Katie couldn't see what the toys were.

She went closer to look.

"Ready?" Sam said to Matt.

"Ready!" Matt yelled.

They both gave a push to the little things on the railing.

Then they went racing down the stairs after them.

When they came back up, Katie saw what the things were.

"Hey!" she yelled. "Stop it."

They were her Beanie Babies! Her sweet little Beanie Babies that they were throwing down the stairs.

Sam was closest to her and Katie reached for him. "Give them to me!" she yelled. She could see that Sam was holding her favorite Beanie, the white cat with blue eyes. "You're hurting them!" she yelled. She tried to grab them.

Sam held the Beanie Babies high, high out of her reach. "I can play with them if I want!" he said.

"Cannot!" Katie said.

"Can too!" he said.

"Hey, Katie!" Matt said.

Katie turned around.

Matt had more of her Beanie Babies. He had them lined up on the railing again. He gave them a big push, and they went flying down the stairs.

"You're hurting them!" Katie yelled.

She went racing down the stairs after them. Matt came racing with her. So did Sam.

"They like it," Matt said. "They're diving into the pool."

"They hate water!" Katie said.

At the bottom of the stairs, Matt tried to get to the Beanies first. So did Sam.

So did Katie.

Matt shoved Katie.

Katie shoved back.

She shoved really, really hard. And Matt went sprawling down.

"Ow!" he yelled. "You hurt me."

Katie bent and gathered up her Beanies.

When she stood up, Mom was standing there. She had Baby-Child on her hip.

Like always. Baby-Child wasn't yelling, though. His mouth was stuffed up with a teething biscuit. He was drooling all over himself and Mom.

"What's going on?" Mom said.

"She pushed me!" Matt said.

He rubbed his elbow, but Katie could see that he was smiling.

She made a face at him. "Matt and Sam were throwing my Beanie Babies down the stairs!" Katie said. "They stole them out of my backpack."

"That's not nice, boys," Mom said.

"Not nice!" Katie said. "Actually, it's awful."

Mom came close to Katie and put her free arm around her. "It's awful," she agreed. "But it's not too nice to push your brother, either."

"He started it!" Katie said.

Mom sighed. "I think you all need to go do your homework now," she said. "How about some quiet time in your rooms, all of you. You can come down when your homework is finished."

"But Mom!" Katie said. "I didn't do anything. And anyway, I don't have any homework."

"Just go," Mom said. "All three of you. To your rooms. And if you don't have homework, then read awhile."

Sam and Matt looked at each other and smiled.

Katie made a mean face at both of them. Then she gathered up her Beanie Babies and her backpack.

Mom stood and waited. She waited while they all turned to the stairs and started up. And that's when Katie saw something, something sticking out of the pocket of Sam's jeans.

It was Beanie Bear, her second favorite Beanie.

"Hey!" she yelled. "Give it here!"

She reached for Sam and grabbed for Beanie Bear. She grabbed hard.

Sam pulled away. Hard.

But Katie was still holding on. And when Sam pulled away, Katie was holding the whole pocket of his jeans in her hand.

12

The Mysterious Word

Another time-out. It wasn't fair. Nothing was fair. And Sam and Matt started it.

Katie slumped down on her bed. She picked up Big Bear again. She held him close to her face. "A whole day of trouble," she whispered to him. "And only bad kids have time-outs."

She heard him say again that she wasn't a bad kid.

She hugged him hard. "I'm not," she said.

But Mrs. Henry thought she was a bad kid that day. And she had written that note to Mom. Katie wondered what the note said.

Katie sat up, reached in her backpack, and took out the note.

It was written in cursive and Katie had a little trouble with cursive. She tried reading it anyway.

It was hard but she found if she read it out loud, she could mostly figure it out. The first line said:

"Katie is very good most of the time. . . ."

"Hey, Big Bear!" Katie said. "It's not a bad note. It's a good note."

She read some more.

It said: "I would like to talk with you about a note I sent last week."

Katie sucked in her breath. Mrs. Henry hadn't forgotten the note.

Katie read some more. The note said: "Lately, Katie seems to be a bit . . ."

Katie frowned. She couldn't read the

next word. Did it say, impossible? Was that the word? Mrs. Henry said that word sometimes when she got frustrated, that people were impossible. Or did the word say something else?

Katie frowned at the word again.

Important? Maybe that's what it said.

No.

Maybe it said she was invisible?

Katie shook her head. No. She wasn't invisible. Hannah was invisible.

Katie screwed up her face. She spelled out the word out loud. I-M-P-U-L-S-I-V-E. Then she tried sounding it out. She sighed. She couldn't figure it out. But whatever it was, she thought it probably wasn't good.

She reread the whole note again. It really wasn't a mean note. It said she was good most of the time. All but that part about I-M-P-U-L-S-I-V-E.

Maybe Mom wouldn't know what it

meant, either. Or maybe, maybe Katie could just erase that part, that word?

Katie stood up and went to her desk. She had a bunch of Magic Markers there and crayons and pencils with erasers.

She picked up her fat pencil with the fat eraser.

But then she thought, no.

But then she thought, yes.

She looked at Big Bear. She asked him if she should erase that word.

Big Bear said no.

She turned her back on Big Bear.

She thought of asking Hannah. But Hannah would probably say no, too.

Katie put down the pencil and eraser. She wished like anything she knew what that word meant.

And then she had an idea! Obie! Obie knew all about words and spelling. Obie was the world's best speller.

Katie opened her door. She looked up and down the hall.

She knew she was supposed to stay in her room for her time-out. But this was important.

Matt and Sam's door was closed. Baby-Child's door was closed. Baby-Child was probably taking his nap.

Obie's door was open. She could see him at his desk, playing on his computer.

She tiptoed down the hall to Obie's room and tiptoed in. "Obie!" she whispered.

Obie turned around. "What?" he said.

"Shhh!" Katie said. She put a finger on her lips. "I'm not supposed to be here," she said.

"How come?" Obie said.

Katie made a face. "Another time-out," she said. She unfolded the note in her hand. "Obie," she said very softly. "What does this mean?" She spelled out the word in the note, "I-M-P-U-L-S-I-V-E?"

"Impulsive!" Obie said. "It means like . . . well, sort of like . . ." Obie screwed up his face. "I think it means, you know, like doing something without thinking first," he said.

"Oh," Katie said. She thought about it. That didn't sound too bad. "Is that a bad thing?" she said.

Obie shrugged. "I don't know," he said. "It doesn't sound that bad to me."

Katie folded up the note and stuck it in her pocket. "That's what Mrs. Henry said I am. I'm that thing, impulsive," she said.

"It's not that bad," Obie said.

Katie sighed. She sat down on Obie's bed and pulled up her knees. There was a fat brown scab on one knee. She picked at the edge of the scab. "Obie?" she said. "How come you never get in trouble?"

Obie shrugged. "I do sometimes."

"Not like me," Katie said.

Obie nodded. He looked sad for her. "I know," he said.

"Is it because you think about things first?" Katie said.

Obie shrugged. "Maybe," he said.

Katie sighed. "I think you think a lot," she said. "I think you think all the time. That's why you're never late or anything."

"I was late once," Obie answered.

"That was my fault," Katie said. She picked at the scab some more. It started to bleed. She rubbed the blood away. "Obie," she said. "Could we play invisible friends?"

"Now?" Obie said.

Katie nodded.

Obie looked at his computer. Katie could see that the screen was filled up with airplanes, all kinds of planes. Obie loved playing airplane games.

He sighed. "Okay," he said. He pushed back from his computer.

"Oh, good!" Katie said. She jumped up from the bed. "Let's play bunnies!" she said. "Let's pretend that Hannah and Jackie find a bunny."

"Two bunnies," Obie said. "Or else they'll fight over who gets the bunny."

112

"Yeah," Katie said. "Two bunnies. But let's pretend their parents don't find out that they have a bunny."

"How come?" Obie said.

Katie shrugged. "Because their parents don't want them to have bunnies," she said.

"Oh," Obie said. "Okay. But I think it would be okay with their parents."

Katie shook her head. She sighed. "No," she said. "I don't think so. I really, really don't."

13

"Is Something Wrong?"

At dinner that night, everybody was very excited. Grandpa would be here for his race this weekend and then he'd be coming back again with Grandma for Easter next week. Sam and Matt were talking about the new video games that Grandpa promised to bring them for Easter. Obie was talking about the airplane computer game Grandpa was bringing him. And Baby-Child was saying his newest word over and over again — truck! Only he said, "Ruck!" Baby-Child loved trucks. He even took his trucks to bed, hugging them like Katie hugged Big Bear. Now, he was running a red plastic dump truck back and forth on his high-chair tray.

"Ruck, ruck!" he said. "Rooom, rooom!"

Katie hardly said anything. She didn't eat much of anything, either. She felt very wiggly in her stomach. She always felt like that when she got worried. All she could think about was that note in her pocket. And that she had that big secret about the bunny.

What would happen when Grandpa came with the bunny? What would Daddy say?

Would Daddy send the bunny away?

Katie had to do something soon. She had to figure it out. Her stomach hurt.

Katie put down her fork and leaned back in her chair.

"What's up, Toots?" Dad said, looking over at her. "You're not eating."

Katie shrugged. "I ate some," she said.

"Not much," Daddy said.

Katie shrugged.

Mom leaned across the table and put a hand on Katie's head, feeling her forehead. "Don't get sick!" she said. She brushed Katie's hair away from her face and smiled at her. "You can't get sick! Easter's almost here," she said.

"I'm not sick," Katie said.

"You look sick!" Matt said. "You look all green." He looked at Sam. "She looks green, doesn't she?" he said.

Sam nodded. "Green and slimy," he said. "Like a lizard."

"Boys!" Mom said. "That's enough."

Katie glared across the table at Sam and Matt. Why did she have to have brothers, anyway?

"At least I'm not a bad kid like you!" she said. "I don't steal people's toys and throw them down the stairs!"

"We didn't steal them," Sam said. "We borrowed them. Beanie Babies like to swim."

"They hate it!" Katie said. "And you were hurting them."

"That's enough, children!" Mom said again. "Let's talk about something nice. I was thinking about our Easter egg hunt this year. I was talking to Grandpa on the phone today. He suggested we have the egg hunt outside this year. Easter is so late and it's so warm out. Would you like that?"

"Where?" Obie said.

"In the backyard," Mom said. "There are so many places to hide things out there."

"Real eggs?" Sam said. "Or candy ones?"

"Both," Mom said.

"I want candy ones," Matt said.

"I want the plastic ones filled with jelly beans," Sam said.

"I think we could have some of each," Dad said.

"So you all like that idea?" Mom said.

Sam and Matt and Obie all said yes, all practically at the same time.

Baby-Child yelled like he was agreeing with them. He waved his truck. He yelled, "Rooom!"

Katie didn't say anything. She was thinking about something. She was coming up with an idea! Mom was right. There were lots of places to hide things in the yard. Way in back was the shed where Katie and Obie had their haunted house last Halloween. They'd almost gotten in trouble for that. But it was a good hiding place, wasn't it? It was far, far back from the house. Hardly anyone went there.

Maybe she could hide her bunny back there. That way, no one would know she had it. Maybe when Grandpa came she could sort of warn him, tell him that when he came on Easter, he could just leave the bunny back there.

"Katie?" Mom said. "You didn't say anything. What do you think about the egg hunt outside? Is that a good idea?"

Katie nodded. "It's okay," she said.

Mom squinched up her eyes at Katie. "Are you sure you feel all right?" she said.

Katie nodded. "I feel fine!" she said.

"Is something wrong?" Mom said.

Katie shook her head. "Nothing's wrong," she said.

She saw Obie look at her. His face was pulled into a big frown, like he was mad. But Katie knew he wasn't mad. He was worried. Obie always looked like that when he was worried.

Katie knew he was worried for her because of that word IMPULSIVE.

"I have a feeling something's wrong," Mom said.

Katie shook her head. "Nothing's wrong!" she said.

"Trouble in school?" Daddy said. His voice was very soft and very nice.

Katie shook her head hard. "No trouble!" she said. "Leave me alone!"

But her voice came out kind of wiggly. And water came to her eyes.

Suddenly, it got very quiet at the table. The boys got very quiet. Even Baby-Child stopped slamming his truck around.

"Katie?" Daddy said. "Look at me. What's wrong?"

Katie just shook her head. She didn't look at him and she didn't answer.

"Katie?" Sam said. "If it's Beanie Babies, we were just fooling."

"Yeah, Katie," Matt said. "We didn't mean to hurt them. I won't touch them ever again, promise."

Katie blinked hard. She could feel the tears coming up to her eyelids. They were going to spill over.

She breathed in very deep and slow to try and hold them back. She blinked very hard.

It was still very quiet in the room.

"Katie?" Sam said. "You don't look green. That was just a joke."

"And you don't look slimy like a lizard, either," Matt said. "You look nice."

Katie looked up. She looked at Matt.

She looked at Sam. She looked at Baby-Child.

They were all looking back at her, worried-looking.

She looked at Obie. He looked super-worried.

She didn't look at Mom or Daddy.

She looked down at her lap.

She dug the note out of her pocket.

"Katie?" Daddy said. "Come and sit on my lap."

He pushed his chair back from the table to make room for her. He patted his lap. "Come on," he said. "Let the best girl in the world come sit on my lap."

Katie stood up. She had the note in her hand.

She went around the table to Daddy.

He reached out and gathered her in.

"That's my girl," he said. He hugged her really close. "The best place for the best kid in the world," he whispered to her.

But he was wrong. Katie knew he

was wrong. She wasn't the best kid in the world. She wasn't even a pretty good kid.

She was a bad kid. A really, really bad one. And she had a note right here to prove it.

14

The Jump

Next morning, Mom and Dad and Katie had a long talk with Mrs. Henry before school. A long, long talk.

First, they talked about what it meant to be "impulsive." It meant just what Obie said it did, to do things without thinking first. Katie knew she WAS impulsive. She did lots of things without thinking first.

But Mrs. Henry told Mom and Dad what a good kid Katie was, too. Mrs. Henry told about all the good things Katie had

124

learned so far this year, and how much Katie had learned about thinking this year. Like, Katie used to call out without raising her hand. Now, she always raised her hand first. Well, almost always. And she used to be late to school lots. Now, she hadn't been late since February. And she hadn't called Tiffany a crybaby or a big pig in a long time like she used to do.

Katie had to smile at that, but it was a secret smile all to herself. She knew she had called Tiffany a big pig lots of times. But she just said that inside her very own head.

Mom and Dad and Mrs. Henry and Katie all decided she was getting very grown-up and learning a lot about thinking first. She just had to work at it a little harder, they said. Like about not calling Mrs. Pickle old and mean. And about not calling Tiffany invisible. And she had to tell the truth. Like tell that she was the one who had called Tiffany invisible, not Hannah.

Mrs. Henry and Mom and Dad all wanted to know more about Hannah.

Katie just shrugged. What was there to tell? Hannah was her friend, her special invisible friend.

When Mom and Dad left, they gave Katie a big hug. Katie promised she'd try harder. Much, much harder. She felt very, very much happier. Mrs. Henry wasn't mad at her anymore, and Mom and Dad told her they were proud of her that she was really learning how to think.

But Katie still had one worry, one big, big worry.

The bunny.

She still hadn't told Mom and Daddy about the bunny. And she knew asking for the bunny wasn't impulsive. She had thought a lot about how to get a bunny. So maybe impulsive wasn't the only thing wrong about her. Maybe what was wrong about her was that she was a liar.

On the playground at recess, Katie

was swinging high on the swing, thinking about what to do.

Her best friend, Amelia, was swinging high right beside her.

Tiffany was swinging high on the other side of her.

"Look at me, Katie," Amelia yelled over. "I'm a bird!"

"Me too!" Tiffany yelled.

Katie looked over at Tiffany. "You are not a bird," Katie said. "You're a rabbit. A scared rabbit."

"I am not!" Tiffany said. "I'm not scared and I am too a bird."

"Not," Katie said. She looked over at Amelia.

"Look at me," Katie said to Amelia. "I'm a Baltimore oriole."

"What's that?" Amelia said.

"It's a beautiful bird," Katie said. "It's orange and black."

"My dress is blue," Tiffany yelled. "I'm a bluebird."

Katie pretended not to hear Tiffany.

"I'm a Baltimore oriole, too," Amelia said. "Watch me fly!"

She let her swing slow down just a little. She dragged her feet to slow it some. And then she jumped.

She flew out over the sand and landed on her feet. Then she stumbled a little and fell down. She brushed herself off, then stood up and smiled at Katie.

"Now you fly!" she said.

"Okay, watch!" Katie said.

She looked all around the school yard. Kids weren't supposed to jump off the swings. But everybody did. And now, no teachers were looking.

Katie let her swing slow down just a little.

But before she could jump, Tiffany yelled, "Watch me! Watch the bluebird fly."

Katie looked over at Tiffany. Tiffany was going very fast and very high. She wasn't slowing down at all.

"Don't jump!" Katie yelled. "Slow down first."

"Watch!" Tiffany yelled. "Here I go!"

"Slow down first!" Katie yelled again.

Tiffany didn't slow down, though. She pumped once more, higher. And then she went sailing off her swing and out over the sand.

Katie closed her eyes.

She opened them.

Tiffany landed hard. She landed on her feet, right by Amelia. But then she tumbled over on her knees and her hands. And the swing came back and hit her in the back of the head.

She yelled, loud.

Amelia quickly grabbed the swing and stopped its swinging.

Katie slowed her swing way down, dragging her feet. She jumped off her swing and ran to Tiffany.

Amelia was bending over Tiffany.

"Are you okay?" Katie asked.

Tiffany shook her head. "No!" she said.

"Where does it hurt?" Katie said. "Let me see."

Tiffany held her knee. Then she touched the back of her head. Then she held her knee again.

Katie looked at Tiffany's knee. It was all scratched up. It was bleeding and there were sand and pebbles stuck in the scratch. It looked very, very yucky.

"Ow!" Katie said. "Does it hurt lots?"

Tiffany nodded. She sniffed hard.

"Does your head hurt?" Amelia asked.

Tiffany nodded. "Not that much," she said. "My knee hurts lots, though." She looked up at Katie. "I wasn't scared to jump," she said.

"That's good," Katie said. "But you should go to the nurse."

Tiffany shook her head no.

"She has Band-Aids," Katie said.

"She'll wash your knee and stick Band-Aids on it."

Tiffany just shook her head again. Katie could see that Tiffany was trying hard not to cry. And Tiffany was usually a big crybaby.

"The nurse has lollipops," Katie said.

Tiffany shook her head even harder.

"How come?" Katie said.

Tiffany sniffed really, really hard. "She'll know I jumped," she said.

Katie could see there were tears in Tiffany's eyes.

And Katie knew it wasn't just being hurt. It was being in trouble. Tiffany never got in trouble.

"Maybe the nurse won't even ask what happened," Katie said.

"What if she does?" Tiffany said.

Katie frowned down at the ground. She thought hard. But she wasn't thinking about Tiffany. She was all of a sudden thinking about something else. She was thinking about herself. She was thinking about telling the truth. She was especially thinking about the bunny.

Katie looked at Tiffany. She sighed. "I guess you probably have to tell the truth," Katie said.

Tiffany sniffed again, but she nodded.

Katie reached down and took both of Tiffany's hands. She pulled Tiffany to her feet. She smiled at Tiffany. It wasn't a mean smile, either. "Come on," she said. "It's not that bad. I'll go with you."

15

The Good Kid

It was Saturday and Grandpa had come for his race. He had run the race early in the morning, before Katie was even up. And he had won, too!

Now it was afternoon, and Katie and Grandpa were going to the playground together, just the two of them.

Katie felt very, very happy to be with Grandpa. And just a little worried in her stomach, too.

Because she had something she had to do.

She had two of her Beanie Babies tucked in her pockets, the two rabbits. She kept rubbing the rabbits' fur.

She and Grandpa walked to the playground, hand in hand.

"Isn't spring a wonderful time, Katie?" Grandpa said as they climbed the steps to the playground. "It always makes me want to sing or something."

Katie laughed. "Why would you sing?"

Grandpa shrugged. "Because I'm happy. Don't you sing when you're happy?"

Katie shook her head. "I laugh when I'm happy," she said.

"Oh," Grandpa said. "Well, I guess I laugh, too. But I sing, too."

He looked around the playground. "Look around!" he said. "Isn't it beautiful?"

Katie looked. It was beautiful out. The sun was shining. Tulips and daffodils were out all over the place. The leaves were coming out and two trees on the playground had pink flowers all over them. The big tree over the swing already had tiny green leaves on it. And Katie could hear a bird singing.

"Hear that?" Grandpa said. "I think birds sing because they're happy. Do you think so?"

"I think so," Katie said. She went over to the sandbox and sat down on the wooden edge.

Grandpa came and sat down beside her.

Katie scooped up a handful of sand. She began dribbling some sand down on an ant that was crawling across the sand.

"So, Toots," Grandpa said. "You excited about Easter?"

Katie shrugged. "Sort of," she said.

"Just one more week," Grandpa said. "We're going to have such fun. An egg hunt out of doors. And some great presents."

Presents.

Katie took a deep breath. She swallowed hard. She had to tell him.

"Grandpa?" she said. "You know my present? The rabbit?"

"I sure do," Grandpa said.

"Well," Katie said. "I've changed my mind. I don't want a rabbit for Easter anymore."

"You don't?" Grandpa said. His voice sounded very surprised. "How come?"

Katie dribbled sand on another ant. "Just because," she said.

"Oh," Grandpa said. "But there must be a reason, right?"

"I don't like rabbits anymore," Katie said. She said it so softly, she wasn't even sure Grandpa could hear her.

But he did hear.

"Oh," he said. "Really? How come? Rabbits are such lovely creatures."

Katie shook her head. "They're not," she said. She thought of what Mrs. Pickle had said about rabbits being very dumb. Katie didn't really believe Mrs. Pickle. But she had to say something.

"They're very dumb creatures," Katie said.

Grandpa laughed. "But soft and sweet," he said.

Katie didn't answer. But she could feel water come to her eyes.

"Katie?" Grandpa said. "Is that the whole reason?"

Katie wanted to say the words. She really, really did. But it was hard.

She looked up at Grandpa. She took a big breath and then she did do it, said the words. They came out all in a big rush.

"See," she said, "I'm not allowed. I told you I was, but I'm not. Daddy said no, and I didn't ask Mom but Mom always says the same thing that Daddy says, so I can't have a bunny. But I really, really want one, but I can't. So don't get me one, okay?"

Grandpa nodded. He took a long, big breath, just like Katie had done. And then he said, "Okay." But he sounded very, very sad when he said it.

Katie made a sad face back at him. "You like bunnies, too, don't you?" she said.

Grandpa nodded. He screwed up his face. "I love bunnies," he said. "I told you, I always wanted one when I was your age."

Katie nodded. She looked down into the sandbox. She was thinking very much. She felt sad about the bunny. Very, very sad. But a little bit happy, too. Happy because she wasn't a bad kid. She was a good kid, just like Daddy said. She had told the truth, even though it was hard. And even though it made her sad.

She felt bad, though, that it made Grandpa sad.

She looked up at Grandpa. "Grandpa?" she said. "If you love bunnies, why don't you get a bunny? For yourself? Your very own bunny?"

Grandpa made another of those sad faces. "I could, I guess," he said. "But I don't know. I think a bunny might get lonely without a little girl to play with."

Katie thought about that. She thought hard. And then she had an idea. She looked up at Grandpa.

"I know!" she said. "I could come visit your bunny."

Grandpa started to smile. "Why, that's right!" he said. "You could!"

Katie smiled back at him. "And know what else?" she said. "You could bring it when you come visit me!"

"I could, couldn't I?" Grandpa said. He was smiling bigger than ever, a big, big smile. But then his face got worried-looking again. "But what would I name it?" he said. "I'm not good at names."

Katie smiled. She had already thought about that. She knew just what she'd name a bunny. "I'm good at names," she said. "We'd name it Hoppy. Hoppy the bunny. And if you got him by Easter time, his name would be Hoppy Easter."

"What a good idea!" Grandpa said. "Think if I got a bunny, I could bring him next weekend? For an Easter visit?"

"Sure!" Katie said. And then she added, "Well, ask Daddy first."

"Oh, I will," Grandpa said. "But I know he'll say yes. After all, it's just a visit. It's not like Hoppy would be living with you."

"Right," Katie said. "Not like that at all."

Grandpa nodded. "He'd just be visiting," he said.

"Right," Katie said. "But it's almost like living with me, right? I can pet him and play with him and feed him and everything, right?"

"Right," Grandpa said.

Katie took a big breath. She smiled at Grandpa.

He smiled back at her.

She started to laugh.

"What?" Grandpa said.

"I'm happy," Katie said.

"I'm happy, too," Grandpa said.

Katie took another big breath. She was happy. She was a good kid. She could have her own bunny — almost. Her own visiting bunny.

She looked down into the sandbox.

The ants she had buried had escaped. They were creeping up the side of the sandbox. She wondered if they were happy to escape. She wondered if they were as happy as she was. She watched them get farther and farther up the side of the box. She started to dribble more sand on them.

But then she decided to leave them alone.

LITTLE 🍎 APPLE®

Here are some of our favorite Little Apples.

There are fun times ahead with kids just like you in Little Apple books! Once you take a bite out of a Little Apple—you'll want to read more!

Reading Excitement for Kids with BIG Appetites!

- ☐ NA45899-X **Amber Brown Is Not a Crayon**
  Paula Danziger $2.99
- ☐ NA93425-2 **Amber Brown Goes Fourth**
  Paula Danziger $2.99
- ☐ NA50207-7 **You Can't Eat Your Chicken Pox, Amber Brown**
  Paula Danziger $2.99
- ☐ NA42833-0 **Catwings** Ursula K. LeGuin $2.95
- ☐ NA42832-2 **Catwings Return** Ursula K. LeGuin $3.50
- ☐ NA41821-1 **Class Clown** Johanna Hurwitz $2.99
- ☐ NA12400-9 **Five True Horse Stories**
  Margaret Davidson $2.99
- ☐ NA43868-9 **The Haunting of Grade Three**
  Grace Maccarone $2.99
- ☐ NA40966-2 **Rent a Third Grader** B.B. Hiller $2.99
- ☐ NA41944-7 **The Return of the Third Grade Ghost Hunters**
  Grace Maccarone $2.99
- ☐ NA42031-3 **Teacher's Pet** Johanna Hurwitz $3.50

Available wherever you buy books—or use the coupon below.

- -

SCHOLASTIC INC., P.O. Box 7502, 2931 East McCarty Street, Jefferson City, MO 65102

Please send me the books I have checked above. I am enclosing $ _____ (please add $2.00 to cover shipping and handling). Send check or money order—no cash or C.O.D.s please.

Name_____

Address_____

City_____State/Zip_____

Please allow four to six weeks for delivery. Offer good in the U.S.A. only. Sorry, mail orders are not available to residents of Canada. Prices subject to change.   LA996